HOUSE OF FEAR

BY
TONY NORMAN

ILLUSTRATED BY
ALEKSANDER SOTIROVSKI

KU-514-310

Titles in Full Flight With Attitude

Hard Drive Boy	Jonny Zucker
Robot Safe Crackers	Jonny Zucker
Blood Wheels	Stan Cullimore
Surf Attack	Alison Hawes
The Dream Catcher	Jane A.C. West
Framed!	Jillian Powell
House of Fear	Tony Norman
Go-Kart Crazy	Roger Hurn
Spirit Tribe	Melanie Joyce
Lunar Rover	David Orme

Badger Publishing Limited
Oldmedow Road, Hardwick Industrial Estate,
King's Lynn PE30 4JJ
Telephone: 01438 791037

www.badgerlearning.co.uk

2 4 6 8 10 9 7 5 3 1

House of Fear ISBN 978-1-84691-667-0

Text © Tony Norman 2009
Complete work © Badger Publishing Limited 2009
Second edition © 2015

ST. HELENS
COLLEGE

NOR

135060

Jan 2016

LIBRARY

All rights reserved. No part of this publication may be reproduced, stored in any form or by any means mechanical, electronic, recording or otherwise without the prior permission of the publisher.

The right of Tony Norman to be identified as author of this Work has been asserted by him in accordance with the Copyright, Designs and Patents Act 1988.

Series Editor: Jonny Zucker
Publisher: David Jamieson.
Editor: Danny Pearson
Design: Fi Grant
Cover illustration: Aleksander Sotirovski

HOUSE OF FEAR

CONTENTS

Badger
L E A R N I N G

CHAPTER 1
DID I KILL HER?

She was dead.

The girl was dead and the four words that rang out in Dino's mind made him feel sick.

"Did I kill her?"

Dino was hard.

It took a lot to scare him, but now his blood ran cold in the House of Fear.

The girl lay at the foot of the stairs.

Dino had chased her, then she fell.

Head over heels. Dino saw her head hit the hard steps on the way down.

"I didn't push her!" he said out loud. "If she is dead, it's not down to me."

It had been a long night and the worst was yet to come...

Chapter 2
Uncle Joe

Dino's dad had left him and his mum a few months before.

The shock hit Dino hard. He felt angry and took it out on his mum. He knew he was out of order, but he did it just the same.

Then one day he gave his mum such a hard time, he made her cry.

That was when Uncle Joe came over for a talk.

"You can't go on like this Dino," Uncle Joe said.

"It's not fair on your mum."

"Dad was sick of her," snapped Dino. "That's why he left us."

"The truth is, we don't know why he left. I'm his brother, but he didn't tell me. What he did was wrong. You've had a hard time son, but so has your mum. She needs your help now."

Dino hung his head. He knew his uncle was right.

He liked Joe. He was a good man.

"OK," said Dino. "I'm... I'm sorry. But I hate my life. I feel so mean all the time. My mates don't want to know me. I go to school, come home and watch TV. That's it. I sit there like an old man.

"That's why I get mad, shout at Mum. I take it out on her."

Uncle Joe gave Dino a long, hard look.

Then he smiled.

"You need to get out more, mate!" he said. "I've got an idea..."

Two days later, Dino had a job at Joe's Pizzas in town.

The brightly lit shop was always full of people. No doubt about it, Joe's pizzas were the best in town.

"When we get a call for pizzas, you take them out on your bike," said Uncle Joe.

"You get the cash and bring it back to me. I'll pay you for every hour you work and you get to keep your tips too!"

"Cool," said Dino.

It felt good to be out.

Dino had been sad for so long.
Now it was time to move on.

He had to work hard, but it was fun.
Time flew past.

There was a mean dog at one house. It tried to bite him. The lady at the door felt so bad, she gave Dino a big tip.

"I'm loving this," Dino grinned, as he jumped back on his bike.

Just one more red, green and white pizza box to deliver.

It had been a great night. Dino had not felt this good in ages.

Then he saw the gang at the end of the alley. There was no way past them.

Their eyes were cold and mean.

Chapter 4
Over In A Flash

Dino knew the six kids from his school.

They went round in a gang, but they did not scare him.

He rode up to Spider, the gang's leader. He was tall and thin.

He was a bully who felt big when he had his mates with him.

"What d'you want?" said Dino in a low voice.

"Give us the cash you got for the pizzas."

"You want it, you take it," snapped Dino.

Spider got hold of Dino's bike.

Dino flew at him in a rage and threw him to the floor.

"Come on, get up," shouted Dino.

Spider did not say a word. His mates stood back. Did they want to fight?

Dino did not wait to find out.

He jumped on his bike and was out of there.

It was all over in a flash.

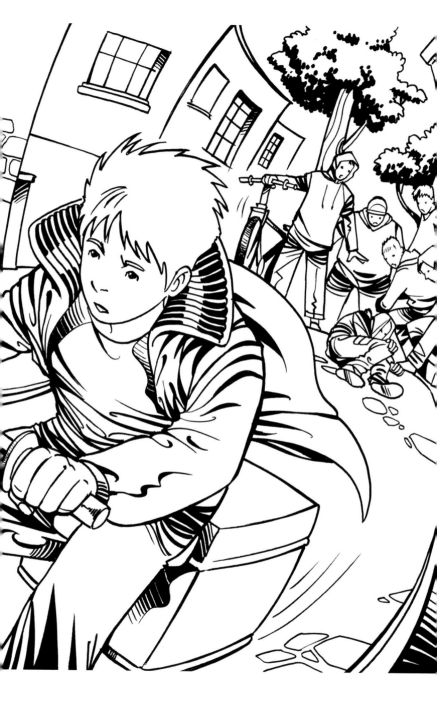

Chapter 5
Into The House of Fear

Dino heard one of the gang shout as he sped out of the alley.

"Come on, let's get him!"

Dino had to get away. His mind was racing as fast as his bike.

He needed a place to hide, but where? Then he saw a big old house he knew well.

Kids at school called it the House of Fear.

They said there was a ghost in there.
Dino turned sharp left into the garden.
It was full of trees and bushes.

He hid his bike and looked up at the
house. It was scary. Dino felt his heart
beat faster.

Was that a face at the window?
A ghost maybe?

"Get real."

Dino spat the words out, but he was
scared and that made him angry.

Angry at the gang who were after him.
Angry at those dumb ghost stories.

Fury rose in him like a fire. He ran at the house and kicked the front door.

The door flew open.

Out on the street, Spider and his gang saw Dino rush inside. They were closing in fast...

Chapter 6
A Trick?

It had the right name for sure.

It was cold and gloomy in there. All the rooms were empty.

Dino heard his feet echo on the bare floor as he looked for a place to hide.

He ran up the dusty stairs.

Soft light came from a room at the front of the house.

Dean stood very still. He was past fear now.

"Who's there?" he shouted.

There was no reply. Dino ran into the room and saw a girl with long blonde hair by the window. She shone with blue light, like a ghost.

"What is this? A trick?"

Dino's voice was hard and cruel. His mind was in a spin. What was all this crazy stuff?

He wanted the girl to tell him. He tried to grab her, but she ran past him.

He chased her to the top of the stairs, then she fell.

"I didn't push her!" said Dino. "If she is dead, it's not down to me."

Chapter 7
The Ghost Girl

"Who's he talking to?" asked
Spider. "I told you he was a freak."

The gang were looking into the house
through a dirty window.

They could see Dino on the stairs, but
not the girl on the floor.

"Come on," said Spider. "Let's get him!"

The gang ran in through the open door.
Dino saw them from the stairs. He
knew there was no way out.

"Wanna fight, do you?" yelled Spider.

"Well, we're ready for you this time!"

He sounded excited. This time he knew he would win.

Then the ghost girl rose up into the air and started to howl.

"You're all freaks. Get out! Get out!"

The gang were shocked.

The ghost's wild, angry voice cut into them like ice.

"Let's go," yelled Spider.

They ran out into the street.

Now it was quiet. Very quiet.
Dino did not know what to say.

"Yes, I am a ghost," said the girl.
"It can get lonely here, but tonight was the most fun I've had in years.

"Did you see their faces? Losers!"

Chapter 8
Fab Pizza

The girl smiled at Dino.

"The last time I ate was in 1967, but I feel hungry now."

"Pizza?" asked Dino. He felt like he was in a dream.

"Fab."

Dino gave her the spare pizza he had left in his bag.

The girl held the box in her hands. It snapped open and the pizza flew up to her mouth.

It was gone in two seconds flat.

"How did you make it look like she can fly?"

The voice came from the shadows.

Spider was back, but not for long.
The ghost girl flew at him screaming.

"I told you to get lost. Now you've got me really mad!"

The ghost dived into Spider's chest and burst out of his back.

She turned into a giant spider and trapped him in her web.

He cried for mercy, but the ghost
howled with cruel laughter.

With a wild flash, the web was gone
and Spider was in a tank of cold water.

The ghost was now an octopus. She
grabbed his head and face with her
eight long legs and started to squeeze
the life from him.

"Stop it!" Dino's voice rang with fear.
"You'll kill him."

Another flash of light and the water and octopus were gone.

"Why did you stop me? I was just having fun!"

The ghost girl laughed, then looked at Spider as if he was dirt.

"You still here?" she snapped.

Chapter 9
House of Fear

Spider stared back at her. He did not say a word. He was in shock.

The girl pointed to the door out onto the street.

"Get out!" she snapped.

Spider ran out into the cold night.

"He won't be back in a hurry," said Dino.

"No," said the girl, "but you can come back any time you want. Bring a pizza, OK?

"Just because I'm a ghost, doesn't mean I can't have friends!"

Dino felt a bit shaky inside. He looked at the girl's strange, smiling face.

"This is crazy," he thought. "I'm not sure I'll be coming here again."

But as he rode home on his bike that night, he knew he had no choice.
He had to go back.

Back to the House of Fear...